Put Beginning Readers on the Right Track with
ALL ABOARD READING™

The All Aboard Reading series is especially designed for beginning readers. Written by noted authors and illustrated in full color, these are books that children really want to read—books to excite their imagination, expand their interests, make them laugh, and support their feelings. With fiction and nonfiction stories that are high interest and curriculum-related, All Aboard Reading books offer something for every young reader. And with four different reading levels, the All Aboard Reading series lets you choose which books are most appropriate for your children and their growing abilities.

Picture Readers

Picture Readers have super-simple texts, with many nouns appearing as rebus pictures. At the end of each book are 24 flash cards—on one side is a rebus picture; on the other side is the written-out word.

Station Stop 1

Station Stop 1 books are best for children who have just begun to read. Simple words and big type make these early reading experiences more comfortable. Picture clues help children to figure out the words on the page. Lots of repetition throughout the text helps children to predict the next word or phrase—an essential step in developing word recognition.

Station Stop 2

Station Stop 2 books are written specifically for children who are reading with help. Short sentences make it easier for early readers to understand what they are reading. Simple plots and simple dialogue help children with reading comprehension.

Station Stop 3

Station Stop 3 books are perfect for children who are reading alone. With longer text and harder words, these books appeal to children who have mastered basic reading skills. More complex stories captivate children who are ready for more challenging books.

In addition to All Aboard Reading books, look for All Aboard Math Readers™ (fiction stories that teach math concepts children are learning in school) and All Aboard Science Readers™ (nonfiction books that explore the most fascinating science topics in age-appropriate language).

All Aboard for happy reading!

For my brand-new nephew, Daniel, who is even
cooler than a pet robot—T.W.

To Grandma Foster—C.R.

Library of Congress Cataloging-in-Publication Data is available.

ISBN 0-448-43282-X (GB)   A B C D E F G H I J
ISBN 0-448-43251-X (pb)   A B C D E F G H I J

The Show-and-Tell Show-Off

By Tracey West
Illustrated by Cindy Revell

Grosset & Dunlap • New York

My name is Reese.

I go to school.

I have a robot.
When I go to school,
Robot stays home.

But then Show-and-Tell day came.
I took Robot to school.

I wanted to show Robot
to all the kids.

I could not wait for my turn!
But first came Lucy's turn.
She had a shell.

Then came Mike's turn.

He had a picture.

Then Mr. Fine said,

"It is your turn, Reese."

"This is my robot," I said.

"His name is Robot."

All of the kids liked Robot.

But not Ben.

"My parrot Polly is better than your robot!" Ben said.

"Polly can fly," Ben said.

"Fly, Polly!"

Polly flew around the room.

"Robot can fly, too," I said.

"Fly, Robot!"

Robot flew up and up.

Then he bumped his head!

All of the kids laughed.

"So what? Polly can talk,"
Ben said. "Talk, Polly!"

"Polly wants a cracker!"
said Polly.

"Robot can talk, too," I said.

I told Robot to say,

"Robot wants a cracker."

But Robot did not say anything.

"What is wrong, Robot?" I asked.
"I DO NOT LIKE CRACKERS,"
Robot said.

All of the kids laughed again.

"So what?

Polly can do tricks," Ben said.

"Do a trick, Polly!"

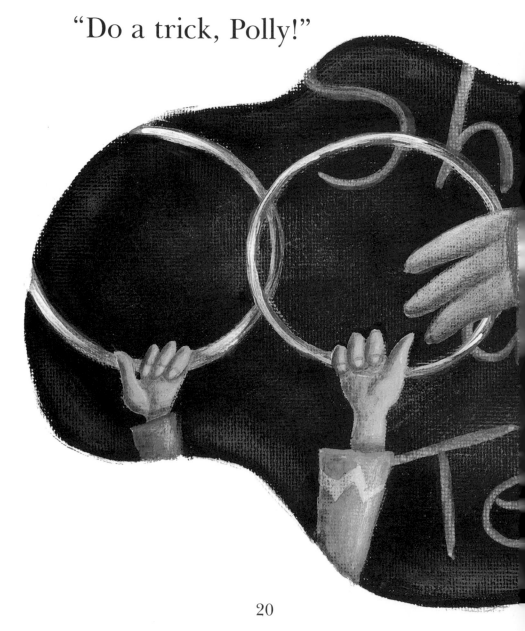

Polly flew through some hoops.

It was a cool trick.

All of the kids clapped.

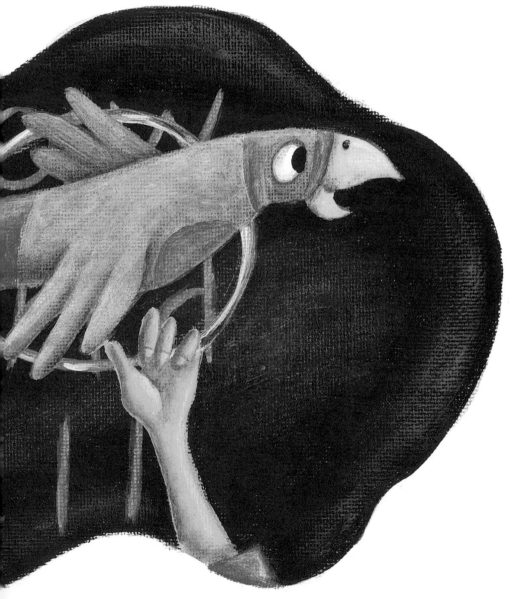

"I CAN DO TRICKS, TOO,"
said Robot.
Robot tried to fly through
the hoops.

He did not fit!
The kids laughed and clapped
for Robot anyway.

"So what?
Polly can spell words,"
Ben said.
"Spell, Polly!"
Polly spelled her name.
"P-O-L-L-Y," said Polly.

"Robot can spell words, too,"
I said.

"Spell, Robot!"

Robot spelled his name.

He did it the Robot way.

"So what?" Ben said.

"Polly is better than Robot!"

"No way," I said.

"Robot is better than Polly!"

Mr. Fine stopped us.

"Wait," Mr. Fine said.

"Polly is a good friend to Ben.

Robot is a good friend
to Reese.

Maybe Ben and Reese
can be friends, too."

"POLLY IS A FRIEND,"
said Robot.

"Robot is a friend!"
said Polly.

"Maybe Mr. Fine is right,"
I told Ben.
"Maybe we can be friends, too."
"Maybe we can,"
Ben said.

"SHOW-AND-TELL IS FUN!"
said Robot.